BEDROOM Mayhem

Chance Hansen Pascha Hansen

Keep Smiling

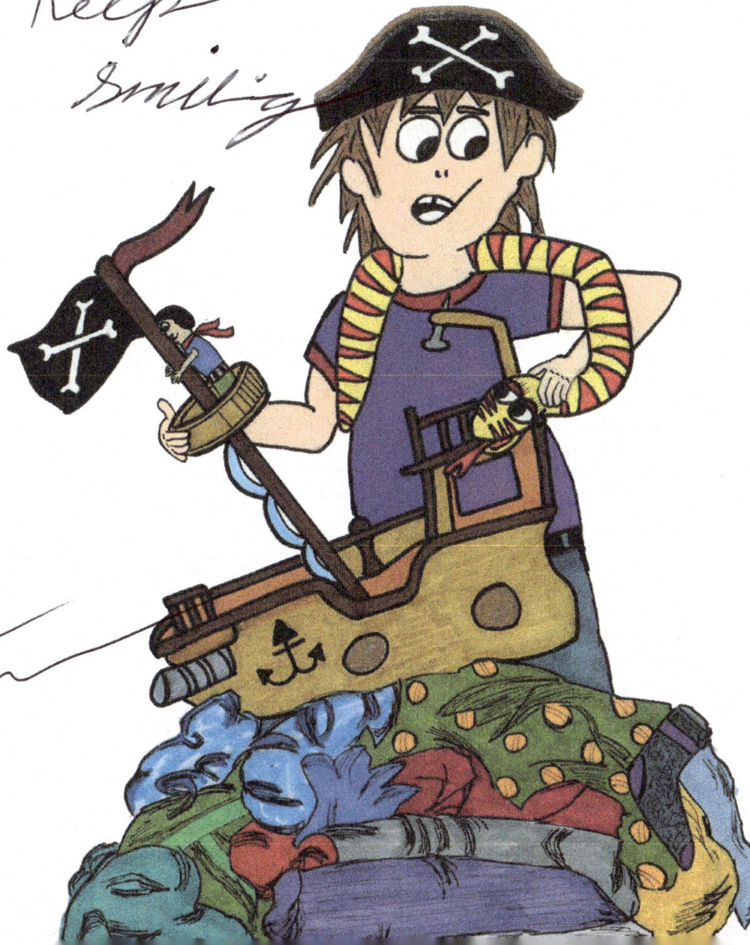

www.trafford.com

North America & international
toll-free: 1 888 232 4444 (USA & Canada)
phone: 250 383 6864 • fax: 812 355 4082

Thank you!

I would like to thank YHVH for all the blessings he's given us and for making this possible. To Pascha Hansen for the awesome illustrations and to Granny and Granddad for all your support. I would also like to thank Trafford for making this possible. I would like to thank all the readers out there, you guys are awesome!

Toby Dreamer stared out the window on a breezy Tuesday afternoon. It wasn't too hot; it wasn't too cold; it was perfect to fly a kite or chase Spooky his pet dog around the yard. He became excited as he watched his friends play outside.

3

Toby looked around. The only problem was that he first had to get out of his room. He took one slow step then another. Suddenly, his leg was stuck on a coat hanger. CRASH! He landed on top of a pile of his stuff on the floor. Then he heard a *thump, thump, thump* from the stairs.

The door jiggled, but it wouldn't open. HHNnuugg. After a couple of moments, the door creaked open. Toby's mother poked her head into Toby's room.

"What a mess! I want this bedroom mayhem cleaned up by dinner!" she said before a stack of mayhem fell, pressing the door closed.

Sitting on the floor, Toby looked at Spooky. "Where does everything go?"

"Whooof!" Spooky replied.

"You're right! All my toys could fit in my closet. I could place the books into my chest and my clothes on the shelves."

He crushed his clothes onto the shelves and jammed his books into his chest before shoving all his toys into his closet. The second he was able to close his stuffed closet, he suddenly he heard *thump, thump, thump* come from the stairs.

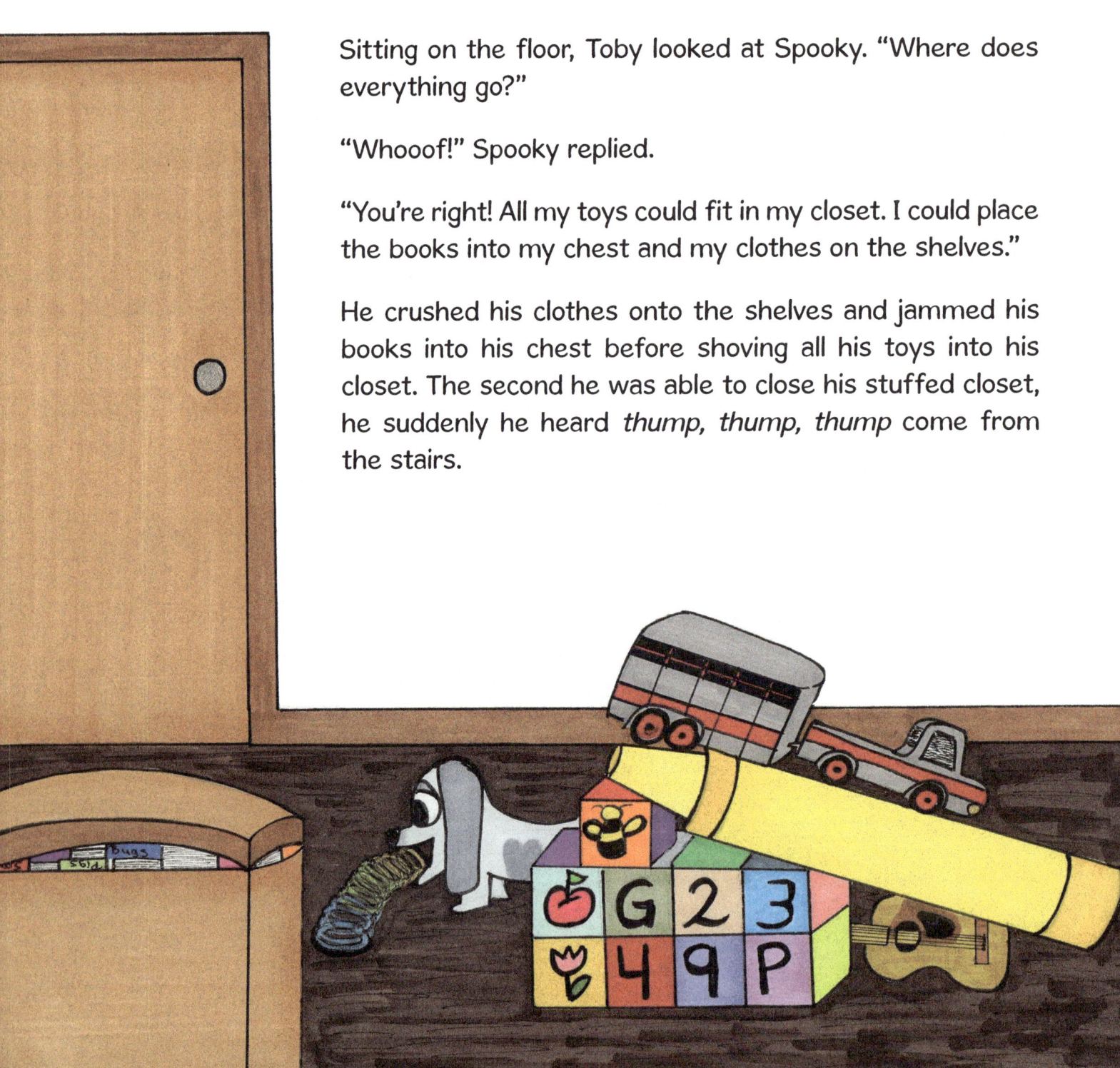

The door jiggled and opened as his father looked into his room.

"It looks good," he said, looking around as he walked toward the closet.

Opening the door, suddenly, a seven-foot-tall tower of toys fell like a crashing wave. At the same time, the chest lid opened as books flew around the room like confetti and Toby's clothes flew off the shelves like they were shot out of a cannon.

Toby's father looked around confused for a moment.

"Look at this mess. You need this bedroom mayhem cleaned up by dinner."

Barely being able to open the bedroom door, he squeezed through a tiny crack, leaving Toby and Spooky to clean up the bedroom mayhem.

Toby Dreamer sat on his floor upset. What could he do? He tried and failed. He found a place for everything, and it didn't work. What could he do? Where could he put all his stuff? Suddenly, he heard a *thump, thump, thump* come from the stairs.

The door opened one inch then another. Suddenly, Toby's sister poked her head into his bedroom.

"What a mess! You're gonna get into trouble with this mayhem."

"I don't understand! I put everything in a place, and it didn't work! How can I clean if it doesn't work? Maybe if I just put everything in a corner of my room . . . Maybe a mostly clean room counts."

Toby's older sister squeezed into his room, saying, "Everything has a place, not put everything in a place. Here, let me show you . . ."

"Only books should be placed on a bookshelf, and only toys placed in a toy chest. See, everything has a place, and it will look best in that place. Cleaning is fast and easy when everything has a place," his sister said as Toby slowly started figuring out where everything's place was.

Suddenly, they heard *thump, thump, thump* come from the stairs.

The door slowly opened before swinging wide open as Toby's mother and father stepped in.

"wow!" they exclaimed as they looked around.

"No chaos, no mayhem—is this really Toby's room?" Toby's mother asked.

As she opened the closet doors, Toby's father hid behind his son, fearing another landslide.

THE END

Take a Chance on another of Hansen's books:

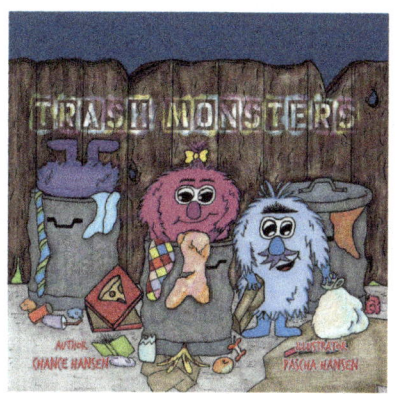

Green Pea, "Not a Home for Me!"
Green Pea Counts One, Two, Three
Green Pea Makes a Flourless Cookie
Green Pea Goes to Salad Bowl School
Green Pea Sings to Me
Green Pea Goes to the Derby

CPSIA information can be obtained
at www.ICGtesting.com
Printed in the USA
LVOW06s0219020217

522920LV00006B/7/P